b.b. cronin

THE

A
SEEK AND FIND
Book

THE

L ST

CHRISTMAS

VIKING

It's Christmas Eve and the children are walking over

to Grandad's house to help him decorate his tree.

Grandad is
taking a break from
decorating.

Happy to see
his grandchildren,
Grandad tells them he
needs their help.
Some of the Christmas
tree ornaments have
gone missing.

Grandad suggests they start searching in the mud room. The red ball, the spinning

rooster, and the green dog ornaments are his favorites. Did he leave them in here?

The rest of the ornaments could be anywhere.

But could any be outside? They don't see any—do you?

Grandad remembers seeing some ornaments in his shed: the rabbit on a sled, the red

lantern, the accordion player, the circus performer, and the man with the green mustache.

While the children search the shed, Grandad looks for his favorite

Santa Claus ornament in the kitchen. He uses his magnifying glass to look closer.

The children come back into the house, and all three start looking in the living room.

Can you help them find the blue bulb, the rainbow bird, the caroler, and the astronaut?

The mail carrier is walking toward the house with a package.

Grandad places the package on a stool to open later when the tree is all decorated.

Right now, he is too busy looking for the green bulb and the yellow snowman ornaments.

Wait
a minute!

Where is
Grandad's
woolly hat?

Back outside they go.

Can you find Grandad's hat?

Grandad has his hat, and they have collected lots of ornaments. But they are still missing

the pink rabbit with the drum, the red bulb, and the green-suited gnome.

The tree looks wonderful,
but one important
ornament is still
missing.

Where is the star?

Better check the living room again from the other direction.

All the ornaments have been found . . .

and some presents, too!

"Merry Christmas to all, and yummm!"

For Esmé, Henry, Ciana, Alison, Sam, Soleil, Nicholas

———

VIKING

Penguin Young Readers

An imprint of Penguin Random House LLC

375 Hudson Street

New York, New York 10014

First published in the United States of America by Viking,

an imprint of Penguin Random House LLC, 2018

LIBRARY OF CONGRESS CATALOGING-IN-PUBLICATION DATA IS AVAILABLE.

ISBN 9780451479044

1 3 5 7 9 10 8 6 4 2

Manufactured in China   Set in Brandon Text

Book design by Mark Melnick

The artwork for this book was rendered with acrylics on paper.

———

Grandad forgot about one ornament!

Can you go back and find this second Santa somewhere in the book?

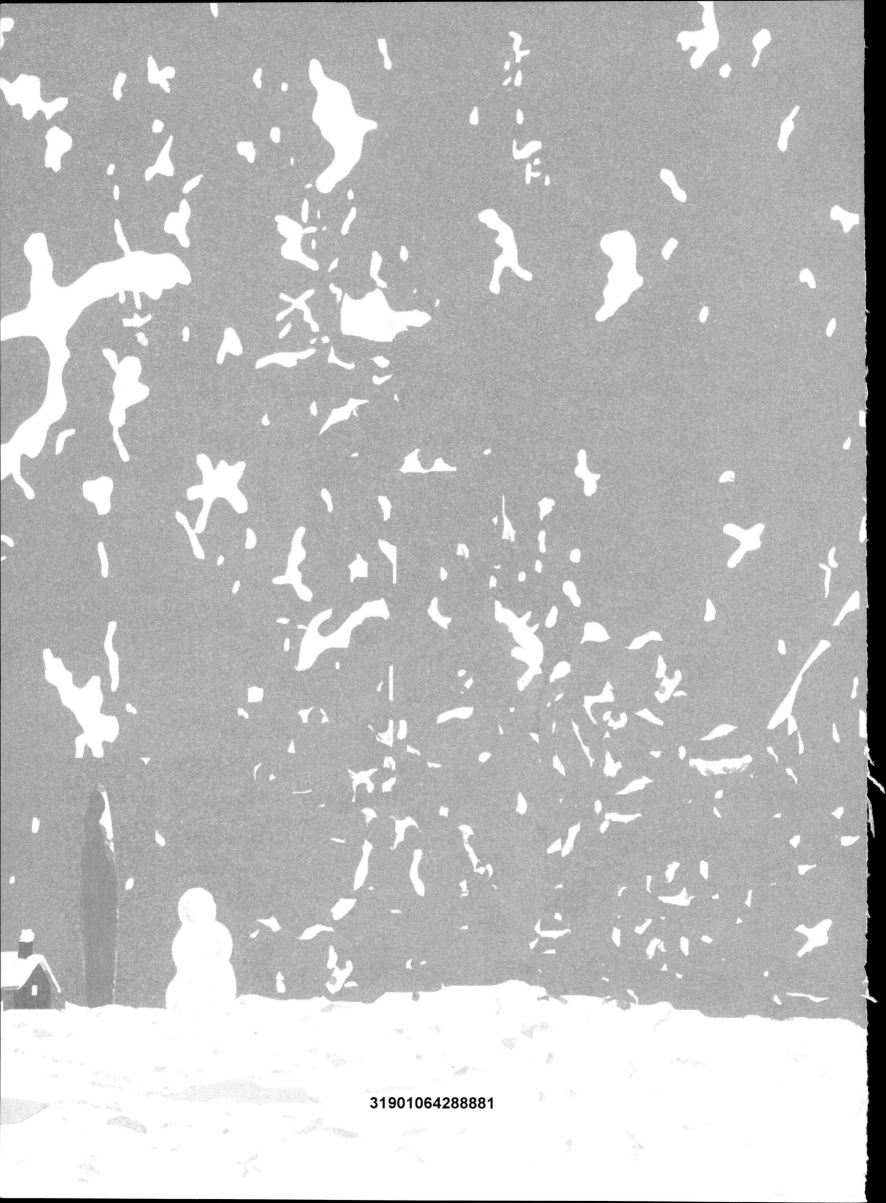